DOWNSIDE
OF DRUGS

Dangerous
Depressants
& Sedatives

DOWNSIDE of DRUGS

ADHD Medication Abuse: Ritalin®, Adderall®, & Other Addictive Stimulants

Alcohol & Tobacco

Caffeine: Energy Drinks, Coffee, Soda, & Pills

Dangerous Depressants & Sedatives

Doping: Human Growth Hormone, Steroids, & Other Performance-Enhancing Drugs

Hard Drugs: Cocaine, LSD, PCP, & Heroin

Marijuana: Legal & Developmental Consequences

Methamphetamine & Other Amphetamines

New Drugs: Bath Salts, Spice, Salvia, & Designer Drugs

Over-the-Counter Medications

Prescription Painkillers: OxyContin®, Percocet®, Vicodin®, & Other Addictive Analgesics

DOWNSIDE of DRUGS

Dangerous Depressants & Sedatives

Celicia Scott

Mason Crest

Mason Crest
450 Parkway Drive, Suite D
Broomall, PA 19008
www.masoncrest.com

Printed and bound in the United States of America.

First printing
9 8 7 6 5 4 3 2 1

Series ISBN: 978-1-4222-3015-2
ISBN: 978-1-4222-3019-0
ebook ISBN: 978-1-4222-8805-4

Cataloging-in-Publication Data on file with the Library of Congress.

Contents

Introduction   7

1. What are depressants and sedatives?   10

2. What are the downsides of sedatives and other depressants?   12

3. What do sedatives look like?   14

4. How are sedatives used?   16

5. What is the history of sedatives?   18

6. If sedatives are dangerous, why are they still legal?   20

7. What other drugs are depressants besides sedatives?   22

8. What do depressants do to your body?   24

9. What do depressants do to your brain?   26

10. Are there "natural" sedatives?   28

11. Are "natural" sedatives less dangerous than other depressants? 30

12. Do teens use sedatives and other depressants?   32

13. How can you tell if someone is
    becoming addicted to depressants?   34

14. Are depressants and crime connected?   36

15. How can depressants affect your future?   38

16. More questions?   40

Further Reading   42

Find Out on the Internet   43

Glossary   44

Index   46

Picture Credits   47

About the Author and the Consultant   48

INTRODUCTION

One of the best parts of getting older is the opportunity to make your own choices. As your parents give you more space and you spend more time with friends than family, you are called upon to make more decisions for yourself. Many important decisions that present themselves in the teen years may change your life. The people with whom you are friendly, how much effort you put into school and other activities, and what kinds of experiences you choose for yourself all affect the person you will become as you emerge from being a child into becoming a young adult.

One of the most important decisions you will make is whether or not you use substances like alcohol, marijuana, crystal meth, and cocaine. Even using prescription medicines incorrectly or relying on caffeine to get through your daily life can shape your life today and your future tomorrow. These decisions can impact all the other decisions you make. If you decide to say yes to drug abuse, the impact on your life is usually not a good one!

One suggestion I make to many of my patients is this: think about how you will respond to an offer to use drugs before it happens. In the heat of the moment, particularly if you're feeling some peer pressure, it can be hard to think clearly—so be prepared ahead of time. Thinking about why you don't want to use drugs and how you'll respond if you are asked to use them can make it easier to make a healthy decision when the time comes. Just like practicing a sport makes it easier to play in a big game, having thought about why drugs aren't a good fit for you and exactly what you might say to avoid them can give you the "practice" you need to do what's best for you. It can make a tough situation simpler once it arises.

In addition, talk about drugs with your parents or a trusted adult. This will both give you support and help you clarify your thinking. The decision is still yours to make, but adults can be a good resource. Take advantage of the information and help they can offer you.

Sometimes, young people fall into abusing drugs without really thinking about it ahead of time. It can sometimes be hard to recognize when you're making a decision that might hurt you. You might be with a friend or acquaintance in a situation that feels comfortable. There may be things in your life that are hard, and it could seem like using drugs might make them easier. It's also natural to be curious about new experiences. However, by not making a decision ahead of time, you may be actually making a decision without realizing it, one that will limit your choices in the future.

When someone offers you drugs, there is no flashing sign that says, "Hey, think about what you're doing!" Making a good decision may be harder because the "fun" part happens immediately while the downside—the damage to your brain and the rest of your body—may not be obvious right away. One of the biggest downsides of drugs is that they have long-term effects on your life. They could reduce your educational, career, and relationship opportunities. Drug use often leaves users with more problems than when they started.

Whenever you make a decision, it's important to know all the facts. When it comes to drugs, you'll need answers to questions like these: How do different drugs work? Is there any "safe" way to use drugs? How will drugs hurt my body and my brain? If I don't notice any bad effects right away, does that mean these drugs are safe? Are these drugs addictive? What are the legal consequences of using drugs? This book discusses these questions and helps give you the facts to make good decisions.

Reading this book is a great way to start, but if you still have questions, keep looking for the answers. There is a lot of information on the Internet, but not all of it is reliable. At the back of this book, you'll find a list of more books and good websites for finding out more about this drug. A good website is teens.drugabuse.gov, a site compiled for teens by the National Institute on Drug Abuse (NIDA). This is a reputable federal government agency that researches substance use and how to prevent it. This website does a good job looking at a lot of data and consolidating it into easy-to-understand messages.

What if you are worried you already have a problem with drugs? If that's the case, the best thing to do is talk to your doctor or another trusted adult to help figure out what to do next. They can help you find a place to get treatment.

Drugs have a downside—but as a young adult, you have the power to make decisions for yourself about what's best for you. Use your power wisely!

—*Joshua Borus, MD*

1. WHAT ARE DEPRESSANTS AND SEDATIVES?

Depressants are drugs. All drugs are chemicals that in some way change the way the body works. Some drugs fight diseases. Other types of drugs change how the body acts in other ways. Some drugs make the body work faster than normal. This type of drugs are known as stimulants. Other types of drugs slow down the body, and these drugs are called depressants. Sedatives are one kind of depressant. They slow down the *central nervous system*, which makes the entire body work slower than usual. The person taking these drugs will probably feel calm and sleepy.

Drugs can help human beings live healthier lives. We think of these types of drugs as medicines. But drugs can also be dangerous when they're not taken in the way they were intended to be used. Even legal, helpful drugs can be deadly when are abused. Sedatives and other depressants can have a very big downside!

These drugs can be dangerous when they're not taken according to a doctor's instructions. The two biggest dangers from depressants are addiction and overdose.

When people are addicted to a drug, the drug is more than a habit. The drug controls their lives. They may stop hanging out with their friends. Nothing seems as important or interesting to them except getting more of their drug. If their addiction goes on long enough, they may lose their friends. They may flunk out of school and lose their jobs.

If someone who is addicted to depressants stops taking the drug, she may have withdrawal symptoms. These range from restlessness, *insomnia*, and *anxiety* to *convulsions* and even death.

An overdose is when someone takes too much of a drug. Because there are many different drugs that are depressants, people may combine them without realizing what they are doing. They can end up over-dosing without knowing. An overdose of depressants can slow the body down to the point that it stops. Sedative overdoses can kill you!

3. WHAT DO SEDATIVES LOOK LIKE?

Sedatives are usually pills. They can be tablets or capsules. They come in many different colors and sizes.

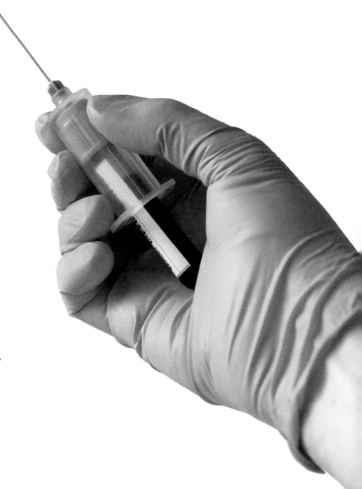

Sedatives can also be given in a hospital setting, or even at your dentist's office. These sedatives can be put directly into your bloodstream with an injection (a shot) or with an *IV* (through your veins). They can even be breathed in as a gas through your nose. When people abuse sedatives, however, they usually take them in pill form.

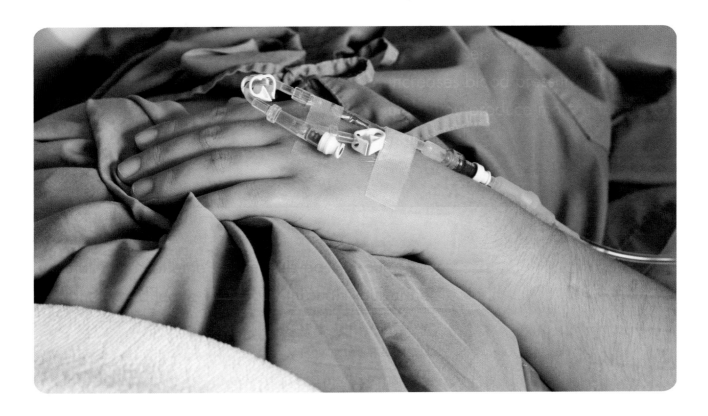

Some sedatives are also called tranquilizers. These are often *prescribed* by doctors to treat anxiety. Other sedatives are called sleeping pills, and people take them when they are having trouble sleeping. Certain kinds of allergy pills can also be sedatives.

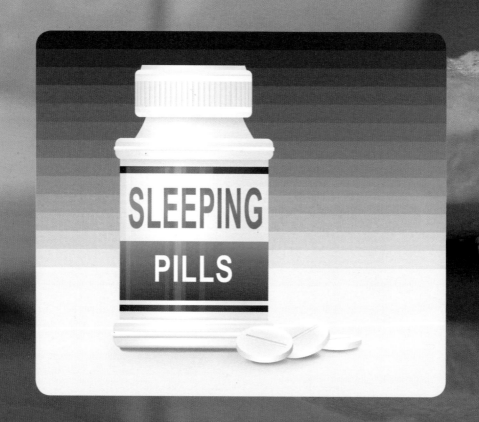

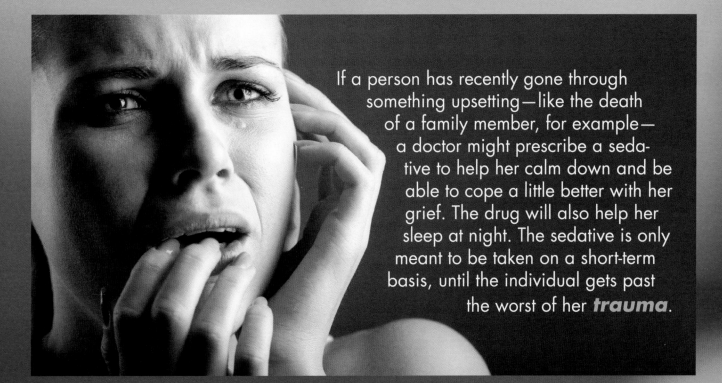

If a person has recently gone through something upsetting—like the death of a family member, for example—a doctor might prescribe a sedative to help her calm down and be able to cope a little better with her grief. The drug will also help her sleep at night. The sedative is only meant to be taken on a short-term basis, until the individual gets past the worst of her *trauma*.

Some people have ongoing problems with anxiety. They may be too anxious to be able to focus on schoolwork or enjoy being with friends. Their anxiety gets in the way of their being able to function well during their daily lives. In those cases, a doctor or *psychiatrist* might prescribe sedatives that are intended to reduce their anxious feelings.

Other people, however, take sedatives without a doctor's prescription—or they abuse the drugs their doctors prescribed. They may share their own prescriptions or their parents' prescriptions with friends. These people take sedatives because they enjoy the feelings of relaxation and happiness they give.

hundreds of years, the only sedatives were alcohol and opium
de from poppies). People used both of these for the same reason
ple use sedatives today:

- to help them relax
- to help them sleep
- to help them cope with pain

- because people liked the
  way these drugs made them
  feel.

hol and opium were abused,
as sedatives are today. And
alcohol and opium-based
s are still being abused.

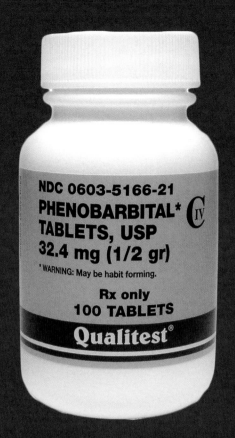

Some new sedatives called barbiturates were created in the nineteenth century. During the first half of the twentieth century, doctors often gave barbiturates to their patients as sleeping pills. Phenobarbitol was one of the most common barbiturates. Doctors still prescribe barbiturates today, but they know now that these drugs can be very dangerous.

Then, in the 1950s, another kind of sedative was developed. These drugs were called benzodiazepines. They were used as sleeping pills, but doctors also prescribed them to people who were feeling upset or anxious. Benzodiazepines were safer than barbiturates. They were less likely to cause addiction, and they had less risk of overdose. The trade names for some common benzodiazepines are Librium, Xanax, Valium, and Halcion. Although these drugs are less dangerous than barbiturates, they can still be abused.

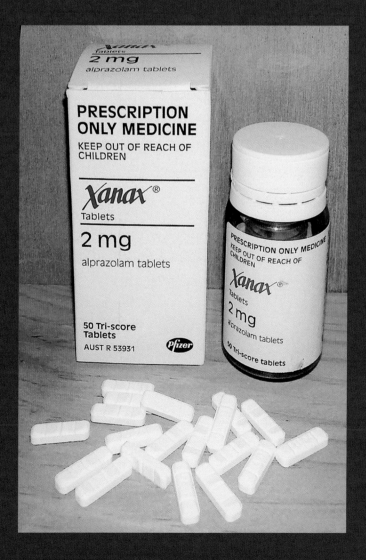

6. IF SEDATIVES ARE DANGEROUS, WHY ARE THEY STILL LEGAL?

When sedatives are used correctly, they can be helpful to people who are in pain or who are terribly upset. Taken properly, they can help with anxiety disorders, which are mental conditions. They can help people deal with upsetting situations. Doctors believe these are useful drugs that help millions of people. Of the people who are given sedatives to treat a medical condition, only a very few become addicted.

When people are in the hospital to have surgery, they are often given sedatives to calm them before they receive *anesthesia*.

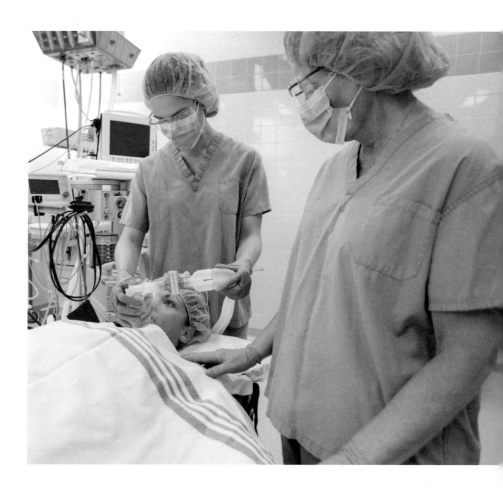

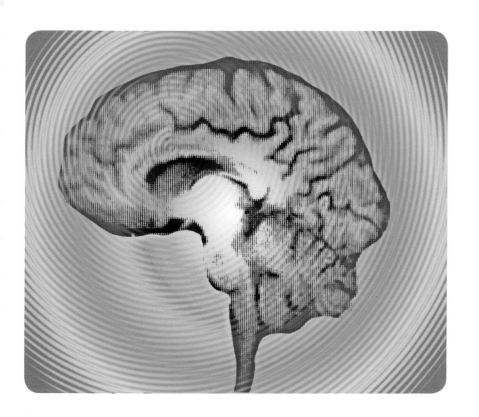

Barbiturates may be prescribed to help prevent *seizures*. During a seizure, the electrical messages passing between nerve cells inside the brain become uncontrolled. Sedatives can stop that from happening.

Depressants are any drugs that slow down your body's nervous system. Marijuana is a depressant, and so is alcohol. Other legal and illegal drugs are also depressants. When any of these drugs are combined— as they often are—they can change and increase the user's reaction.

Medications called antihistamines were developed to counteract allergic reactions. Most of them are available without a prescription. They block the body's histamine response, which is what triggers rashes, runny noses, and other allergy symptoms. But antihistamines are also depressants, so they often have the side effect of making people feel drowsy and foggy.

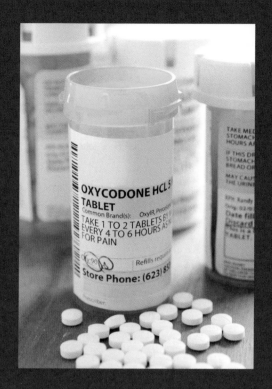

Many prescription-strength painkillers are also depressants. Older drugs such as morphine, as well as newer drugs like oxycodone and hydrocodone, are included in this group. Doctors prescribe these drugs to help their patients cope with pain, but prescription painkillers are also used illegally and *recreationally*. These drugs are addictive—and because they have the power to slow down the body's brain and nerves to such a great extent, the risk of a deadly overdose is high.

Another depressant is a drug called Rohypnol® (flunitrazepam), a type of benzodiazepine. It is not legally prescribed in the United States, but it is available by prescription in other countries. Illegal shipments from Mexico are smuggled into the United States, where it is sold illegally. When Rohypnol is taken recreationally, the pills are often referred to as "roofies." It is sometimes known as a "date rape" drug because of the power it has to make someone unaware of what's going on around her.

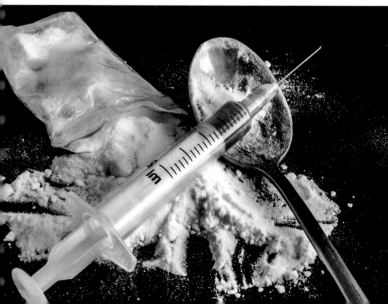

Heroin is a powerful illegal drug that is also a depressant. People use needles to inject themselves with heroin to get high and feel good—but heroin can be deadly. It is extremely addictive, and as it slows down the nervous system, many body organs can be damaged. Heroin destroys people's lives.

8. WHAT DO DEPRESSANTS DO TO YOUR BODY?

Depressants have both short-term and long-term side effects on the body.

Some of the short-term effects include slowed pulse and breathing, lowered blood pressure, tiredness, dizziness, blurred vision and wide pupils, and difficulty with urination. Higher doses can make a person lose his memory of events going on around him. He may not be able to make good judgments, and he may feel **paranoid**. Some people have the opposite response to depressants from what is intended—instead of feeling calm and peaceful, they may become angry, aggressive, and upset.

When depressants are used long-term, the body becomes **tolerant** to them. This means that larger doses will be needed in order to achieve the same effects that lower doses once did. As the user tries to reach the same "high," she may increase her dose to the point that her body slows down too much, causing **coma** or death.

These drugs can also increase the risk of high blood sugar, diabetes, and weight gain (up to 100 pounds). In a recent study conducted by *USA Today*, a type of depressant was linked to forty-five deaths caused by heart problems, choking, liver failure, and suicide.

Side effects of
Alprazolam

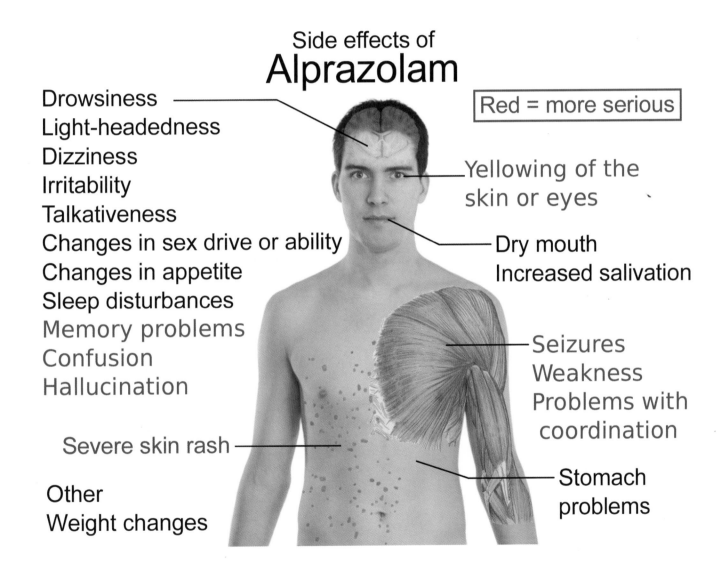

Red = more serious

Drowsiness
Light-headedness
Dizziness
Irritability
Talkativeness
Changes in sex drive or ability
Changes in appetite
Sleep disturbances
Memory problems
Confusion
Hallucination

Severe skin rash

Other
Weight changes

Yellowing of the skin or eyes

Dry mouth
Increased salivation

Seizures
Weakness
Problems with coordination

Stomach problems

9. WHAT DO DEPRESSANTS DO TO YOUR BRAIN?

The nerves inside your brain (and throughout your body) pass messages to each other in long chains. Nerves bring messages from your senses—smell, touch, sight, smell, and sound—to your brain, and then your brain sends messages back to your muscles and other body parts, telling them how to respond. Without this chain of communication between your nerve cells, you wouldn't be able to know what was going on around you. You wouldn't be able to think or move. You wouldn't even be able to breathe.

But between each nerve cell is a tiny gap (called a synapse). The cells need a chemical called a neurotransmitter to carry the messages across these gaps. There are several kinds of neurotransmitters. One of them is called GABA.

Depressants increase the amount of GABA in your body. When there is too much GABA in the nervous system, the messages pass more slowly between the nerve cells.

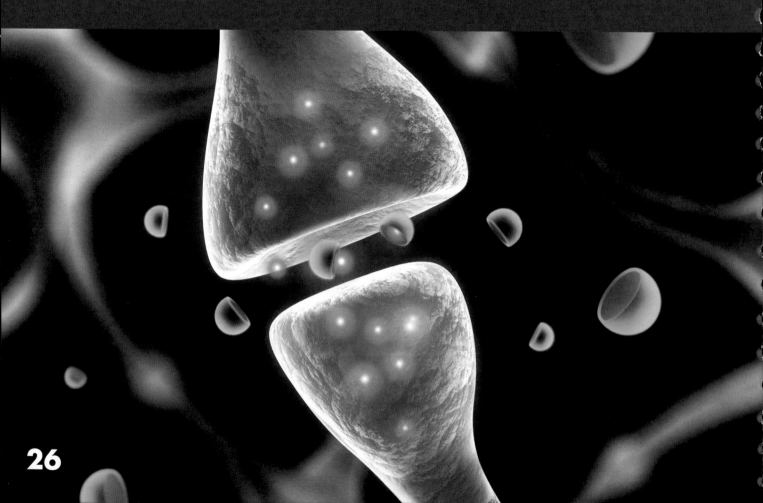

Your senses don't pass messages as clearly to your brain (which is why your vision may be blurry when you take a depressant). Your brain doesn't send messages back to your muscles as quickly, which is why you may become clumsy and uncoordinated. You may have a hard time thinking, because the messages between your brain cells just aren't being passed along normally.

If you take too much of a depressant drug (or a combination of depressant drugs), your nervous system may not be able to work at all. With no messages being passed between nerve cells, the brain shuts down—and when the brain shuts down, so does the body. This is why an overdose of depressants is so dangerous.

10. ARE THERE "NATURAL" SEDATIVES?

"Natural" medications—often called herbal remedies—are substances from plants that people take for their medicinal effects. Many herbal remedies have sedative powers. Some of the most common are shown here.

- St. John's wort

- valerian

- chamomile

- kava kava

- lavender

The leaves, stems, or roots from these plants and others are often dried and then sold as an herbal tea. The plant substances may also be sold in pill or capsule form, or as a liquid. People have been taking them for centuries to relieve pain, calm stressed nerves, and help sleeplessness.

11. ARE "NATURAL" SEDATIVES LESS DANGEROUS THAN OTHER DEPRESSANTS?

Most herbal sedatives are milder than either the legal or illegal depressant drugs. This means their effects on the body are not as strong, so they are not usually dangerous. However, just because something comes from a plant does not mean that it is automatically safe! Natural remedies have a few dangers of their own.

People often take herbal remedies without consulting with a doctor. They may not understand what they are taking, and they may not know what is actually wrong with them. The herbal substance could mask symptoms that would tell a doctor about a treatable illness.

Herbal remedies are not regulated by the government the way other drugs are. This means that you can't be sure how strong the substance is, or even know for sure what's in it. The capsules in one bottle might be much stronger, for example, than the capsules in another bottle made by the same company. This means that people may end up taking more than the correct dosage.

The reason that herbal remedies work is because plants contain chemicals, just as other drugs do. These chemicals can have unwanted side effects. Kava kava, for instance, has been linked to serious illnesses, such as liver damage and nerve damage, and even death. It should never be taken over a long period of time.

The chemicals in herbal remedies can also combine with other drugs in unwanted ways. St. John's wort, for example, can make birth control pills not work. When kava kava is combined with other sedatives, including alcohol, its dangerous side effects become more likely.

Whenever you put anything into your body, even if it's a plant substance, it can have effects that you don't want. That's why it's important to always talk to a doctor about whatever treatments you take, even if they're "natural."

12. DO TEENS USE SEDATIVES AND OTHER DEPRESSANTS?

A 2013 study done of young people visiting hospital emergency rooms found that the answer to this question is yes. About one out of every ten young people between the ages of fourteen and twenty reported that they regularly abuse sedatives and other prescription depressants.

The study also found out these things about young people who abuse sedatives:

- They were more likely to participate in risky behaviors (like speeding while driving, having unprotected sex, and taking other illicit drugs) than other teens their age.
- Their school grades were lower.
- They were more likely to have been hurt in an accident in the past year.
- They were more likely to smoke and abuse alcohol.

13. HOW CAN YOU TELL IF SOMEONE IS BECOMING ADDICTED TO DEPRESSANTS?

A person abusing sedatives may not be conscious of how her drug use is changing her appearance and behavior. The most visible symptoms of sedative abuse or addiction may include:

- looking sleepy or groggy
- being confused about time and surroundings
- involuntary gestures, body movements, and twitches
- rapid eye movement
- poor judgment and decision making
- memory problems

If someone you know has these symptoms, it could mean he needs help!

DANGER

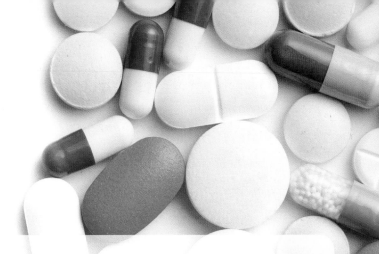

Remember, even sedatives that are prescribed by a doctor can cause addiction. Here are signs that a person is becoming addicted to prescription sedatives:

- frequent requests for refills from physicians, using excuses like lost prescriptions
- stealing or borrowing medication from family and friends.
- using up the medication much faster than the directions indicate
- stealing or forging prescriptions
- ordering prescription medications over the Internet
- the need to take more of the drug to get the same results

Several other behavior patterns often accompany drug addiction:

- mood swings
- changing sleep patterns
- increasing *irritability*, especially when the drug isn't available
- more frequent alcohol use
- spending more and more time focused on getting the drug, while being willing to go to greater and greater effort to get it
- withdrawing from activities that were once enjoyed

CRIME SCENE DO NOT CROSS

CRIME SCENE DO NOT CROSS

Drug abuse and crime almost always go hand-in-hand. The demand for sedatives can trigger robberies of homes, doctors' offices, and drug-stores, and lead from there to illegal *trafficking*. Researchers around the world are also linking sedatives to crime in other ways besides just the sale of these drugs.

- In some areas of the United States, people who have been arrested are now more likely to be abusing benzodiazepines than opiates such as morphine or heroin.

- In Canada, emergency room patients with violence-related injuries were more likely to test positive for benzodiazepines than other emergency room patients.

- Taking some of these drugs may actually make people more likely to commit a crime. Some sedatives take away *inhibitions* and give the user feelings of power and *invincibility*. In this state, the person may be more likely to commit a crime that he would not otherwise have the courage to try. Researchers in the UK found that people who were arrested for shoplifting, property crimes, violence, and driving while intoxicated were also more likely to be on some form of sedatives.

- Research done by the Australian government found that benzodiazepine users are more likely to be violent, more likely to have contact with the police, and more likely to have to have been charged with a crime than people who use heroin and other opiates.

- Benzodiazepines have also been used intentionally by murderers before they kill someone because these drugs give them the sense of power and fearlessness they need to commit murder.

- Rohypnol and other sedatives have been given to people in bars or at parties to make them easier to rob or sexually assault. (Never leave your drink unattended at a party or a bar!)

15. HOW CAN DEPRESSANTS AFFECT YOUR FUTURE?

Young people who become addicted to sedatives don't do as well in school. They're more likely to be absent, and they do poorly on tests and homework. They can't concentrate or remember as clearly as they would normally. This means that they're less likely to be accepted by colleges where they would study for their future careers.

If you're addicted to sedatives, you'll be less able to hold down after-school and summer jobs. Missing lots of days because you're too sleepy to come into work and making lots of mistakes on the job because you're too groggy to think clearly are both good ways to get fired! This can also hurt your chances of getting a good job in the future.

Addiction to sedatives gets in the way of the rest of your life. It can hurt your relationships with your friends and family. It can make you more likely to be involved with a crime. It can keep you from thinking clearly, so that you make bad judgments. Chances are, you will have to live with these for the rest of your life!

What should I do if I think someone has overdosed on sedatives or another depressant?

An overdose is when someone takes too much of any drug or medication, so that it causes serious, harmful symptoms or even death. If you think you or someone else has overdosed on a drug, you should always call 911 immediately. If it's not an emergency but you have questions about preventing an overdose, you can also call the National Poison Control Center (1-800-222-1222) from anywhere in the United States. It is a free call and it's *confidential*. You can call for any reason, 24/7.

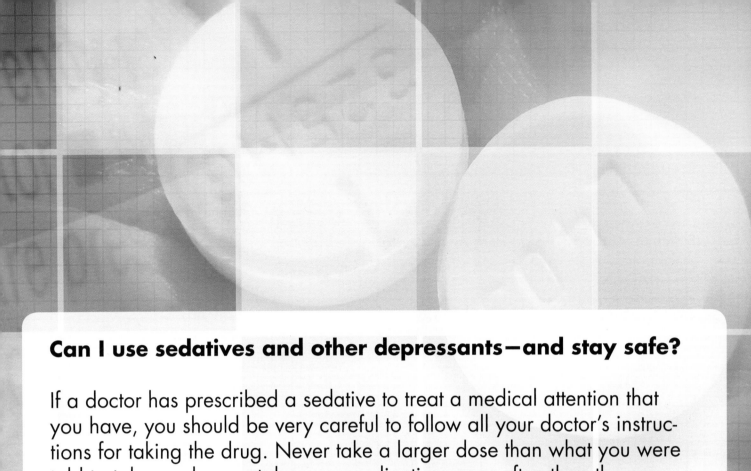

Can I use sedatives and other depressants—and stay safe?

If a doctor has prescribed a sedative to treat a medical attention that you have, you should be very careful to follow all your doctor's instructions for taking the drug. Never take a larger dose than what you were told to take, and never take your medication more often than the prescription tells you. Don't ever combine sedatives with alcohol or other recreational drugs, and be sure to let your doctor know if you're taking any other medicines that could react with the sedatives. If you follow your doctor's instructions exactly, letting her know any concerns you might have, you should be able to safely take this medication.

Taking any drug that you get from a friend or that you find in your parents' medicine cabinet, though, is never safe! Sedatives and other depressants are powerful chemicals. They can make you feel high—but they can also destroy your life. They could even kill you.

FURTHER READING

Breggin, Peter. *Your Drug May Be Your Problem: How and Why to Stop Taking Psychiatric Medications.* Cambridge, Mass.: Da Capo, 2007.

Fletcher, Anne M. *Inside Rehab: The Surprising Truth About Addiction Treatment—and How to Get Help That Works.* New York: Viking, 2013.

Inaba, Darryl S., and William E. Cohen. *Uppers, Downers, All Arounders.* Medford, Ore.: CNS Productions, 2011.

Lyman, Michael D. *Drugs in Society, Seventh Edition: Causes, Concepts, and Control.* Cincinnati, Ohio: Anderson, 2013.

Porterfield, Jason. *Downers: Depressant Abuse.* New York: Rosen, 2007.

Samet, Matt. *Death Grip: A Climber's Escape from Benzo Madness.* New York: St. Martin's Griffin, 2014.

Sheff, David. *Clean: Overcoming Addiction and Ending America's Greatest Tragedy.* New York: Houghton Mifflin Harcourt, 2013.

Tone, Andrea. *The Age of Anxiety: A History of America's Turbulent Affair with Tranquilizers.* New York: Basic Books, 2008.

Walker, Ida. *Sedatives and Hypnotics: Deadly Downers.* Broomall, Penn.: Mason Crest, 2012.

FIND OUT MORE ON THE INTERNET

Barbiturate Overdose
www.nlm.nih.gov/medlineplus/ency/article/000951.htm

Center for Substance Abuse Research: Benzodiazipines
www.cesar.umd.edu/cesar/drugs/benzos.asp

Depressants and Crime
criminal.laws.com/controlled-substances/types-of-substances-often-controlled/
depressants

Neuroscience for Kids: Barbiturates
faculty.washington.edu/chudler/barb.html

Psychology Today: Sedatives
www.psychologytoday.com/conditions/sedatives

Encyclopedia Britannica: Tranquilizers
www.britannica.com/EBchecked/topic/602263/tranquilizer

What Are Sedatives?
www.news-medical.net/health/Sedatives-What-are-Sedatives.aspx

GLOSSARY

anesthesia: Drugs given by a doctor to put you to sleep or numb pain during a medical procedure.

anxiety: A feeling of worry or nervousness.

central nervous system: Your brain and your spinal cord, which work together

coma: Deep unconsciousness that you can't wake up from.

confidential: Kept a secret.

convulsions: Powerful, involuntary muscle movements.

inhibitions: Feelings that keep you from doing something too extreme or scary.

insomnia: A condition where you are unable to fall asleep or stay asleep.

invincibility: Powerful, unable to be be overcome or beaten.

irritability: A tendency to get angry or grumpy easily.

IV: Administering a drug through a needle that goes straight into your vein.

paranoid: Feeling afraid or distrustful of others without a good reason to be.

prescribed: Told to use a drug by a doctor. Certain drugs can only legally be used with a prescription from a doctor.

psychiatrist: A doctor who studies and treats problems with your mind.

recreationally: Done for fun. When used to describe drugs, recreational use is when you use drugs to get "high" instead of as a medication.

seizures: Abnormal electrical activity in the brain that can cause muscle spasms and unconsciousness.

tolerant: Resistant to the effects of something.

trafficking: Illegal buying and selling.

trauma: A disturbing experience or a major injury.

INDEX

addiction 12–13, 19–20, 23, 34–35, 38–39
alchohol 22, 31, 33, 35, 41
anesthesia 21
antihistamines 22
anxiety 13, 16–17, 20

barbiturates 19, 21
benzodiazepines 19, 23, 37
blood pressure 24
brain 21, 23, 26–27

central nervous system 10
chamomile 29
coma 24
convulsion 13
crime 36–37, 39

death 13, 17, 24, 31, 40
diabetes 24
doctor 12, 16–17, 19–20, 23, 30–31, 35–36, 41

GABA 26

Halcion 19
heart 24
herbal remedies 28, 30–31
heroin 23, 37

insomnia 13

kava kava 29, 31

lavender 29
Librium 19

liver 24, 31

marijuana 22
medicine 11, 41
natural 28, 30–31

nerves 21, 23, 26–27, 29, 31
neurotransmitters 26

opium 18
overdose 12–13, 19, 23, 27, 40

painkillers 23
phenobarbitol 19
psychiatrists 17

Rohypnol 23, 37
roofies 23

school 13, 33, 38–39
seizures 21
side effects 22, 24–25, 31
sleeping pills 16, 19
St. John's wort 28, 31
synapse 26

tranquilizer 16

valerian 28
Valium 19
vision 24, 27

weight gain 24

Xanax 19, 25

PICTURE CREDITS

ABOUT THE AUTHOR AND THE CONSULTANT

CELICIA SCOTT lives in upstate New York. She worked in teaching before starting a second career as a writer.

DR. JOSHUA BORUS, MD, MPH, graduated from the Harvard Medical School and the Harvard School of Public Health. He completed a residency in pediatrics and then served as chief resident at Floating Hospital for Children at Tufts Medical Center before completing a fellowship in Adolescent Medicine at Boston Children's Hospital. He is currently an attending physician in the Division of Adolescent and Young Adult Medicine at Boston Children's Hospital and an instructor of pediatrics at Harvard Medical School.